E   Beard, Darleen
          Bailey.

The pumpkin man from
Piney Creek.

$14.00

DATE			

The Pumpkin Man
from
Piney Creek

The Pumpkin Man

from

Piney Creek

by *Darleen Bailey Beard*   *Illustrated by* *Laura Kelly*

Simon & Schuster Books for Young Readers

SIMON & SCHUSTER BOOKS FOR YOUNG READERS
An imprint of Simon & Schuster Children's Publishing Division
1230 Avenue of the Americas, New York, New York 10020

SIMON & SCHUSTER BOOKS FOR YOUNG READERS is
a trademark of Simon & Schuster.

Book design by Carolyn Boschi
The text for this book is set in New Caledonia.
The illustrations are rendered in watercolors.
Manufactured in China
First edition
10 9 8 7 6 5 4 3 2 1

LIBRARY OF CONGRESS CATALOGING-IN-PUBLICATION DATA

Beard, Darleen Bailey.
The pumpkin man from Piney Creek / by Darleen Bailey Beard ;
illustrated by Laura Kelly. — 1st ed.
p. cm
Summary: After seeing a jack-o'-lantern for the first time, Hattie tries
to convince her father to spare one of the pumpkins he is selling.
ISBN 0-689-80315-X
[1. Pumpkin—Fiction. 2. Jack-o'-lanterns—Fiction.]
I. Kelly, Laura (Laura C.), ill. II. Title.
PZ8.3.B374Pu   1995   [E]—dc20   94-34696

For Jacqui Schickling, my fifth-grade teacher, who made me stand up in class and read my stories, and told me one day I'd write a book!

D. B. B.

To Sally S. and George W. Harris, my grandparents, with love.   L. K.

"As I live and breathe."

"My stars!"

"Would you look at that?"

Hattie slipped through the crowd. What was all the commotion about? Standing on tiptoe, she peered between heads and hats.

There, in the storefront, sat a pumpkin. Not the everyday kind of pumpkin that grew in her Pa's field, but a glowing pumpkin with a face.

It had pie-shaped cuts for eyes and nose, a wide smiling mouth, and a candle inside that flickered and danced.

A sign said Jack-o'-lantern. Hattie giggled. Imagine that—a pumpkin named Jack with three crooked teeth!

"Guess what I saw?" Hattie shouted, running into the barn. "A smiling pumpkin named Jack-o'-lantern!"

Ma and Pa looked up, surprised. "Now if *that* don't beat all."

"Pa?" Hattie asked. "Can we make a jack-o'-lantern?"

Pa shook his head. "The Pumpkin Man from Piney Creek is coming out tomorrow. Says he has a store that'll buy every pumpkin we've grown, if they're good enough."

At supper time, Hattie helped Ma set the table, filling their plates with beans and corn bread.

Pa rubbed his belly and growled like a hungry bear. But Hattie didn't laugh, her mind still on pumpkins.

"Can't we keep just *one*?" she begged. "Please?"

"We already have a four-pie pumpkin in the cellar," Pa said, sopping his bread in molasses. "Ma's going to make her blue-ribbon pies for Thanksgiving."

Hattie's mouth watered, remembering Ma's creamy pies. "But can't we keep one for pies and one for a jack-o'-lantern?"

"Sorry, Hattie-Pattie."

Early the next morning, Pa and Hattie walked to the pumpkin field, their breath fogging the air. Pa cut vines and Hattie rolled pumpkins into heaping golden piles. They worked their way from east to west, leaving mounds of morning-wet pumpkins behind them.

Into the afternoon, Hattie rolled and pushed and shoved. Just when she thought her back would break, she spied the *perfect* pumpkin. Just the right size for a jack-o'-lantern. Surely Pa wouldn't miss it.

She quickly covered it with dry vines, then marked the spot with two sticks and went back to rolling and stacking pumpkins.

"Whoa!" hollered the Pumpkin Man from Piney Creek. His wagon creaked to a stop and he jumped off his high-spring seat.

"'Tis a great pumpkin day!" he boasted, tipping his fine beaver hat. He shook hands with Pa, then held out his hand to Hattie.

"Lands o' mercy," he said, pulling a raspberry cream right out of her ear.

Hattie giggled and crunched the sweet candy, while he and Pa inspected each heap, wheeling and dealing and talking pumpkins.

The Pumpkin Man cut a pie shape into one of the pumpkins, then pulled out its orange flesh. He held it up to the sun, smelled it, tasted it, and looked at several seeds.

Pa and Hattie held their breath, hoping he'd be pleased.

"Best I've found," the Pumpkin Man announced. "How many do you have?"

"Exactly one hundred," Pa said.

Hattie drooped. Pa had been counting! Was *her* pumpkin part of Pa's hundred?

"I'll buy them all," the Pumpkin Man said.

Pa slapped his knee and whistled, but Hattie kept silent. Turning her face from Pa, she helped load the wagon.

As early-evening shadows stretched from tree to tree, the wagon sat heaping high. The field lay empty and bare—except for one perfect pumpkin.

"'Tis ninety-nine," the Pumpkin Man counted. "Where's the last one?"

Pa's eyes scanned the field. He looked under the wagon, then kicked a clod of dirt and headed for the cellar.

"No, Pa!" Hattie trembled. "Don't sell Ma's pumpkin!"

"I'm a man of my word," Pa shouted. And he disappeared into the ground.

Hattie ran to the spot marked by two sticks. Tossing aside the vines, she grabbed her secret pumpkin.

"Here," Hattie cried, tears stinging her cheeks. "Maybe someone in Piney Creek will make a jack-o'-lantern with it."

"Is that what *you* aimed to do with it?" the Pumpkin Man asked.

Hattie looked at the ground. Ashamed, she nodded her head.

Just then, Pa topped the cellar, Ma's pumpkin in his arms.

"Never mind!" the Pumpkin Man called. He winked at Hattie. "I've a hundred after all!"

Reaching into his vest, the Pumpkin Man pulled out a leather bill book, thick with money. He counted six bills into Pa's hand. "Always a pleasure doing business," he said, tipping his hat once again.

Pa hurried inside to show Ma their money. Hattie sat on the stoop, hugging her knees in the night air, while the Pumpkin Man hopped onto his high-spring seat.

But the Pumpkin Man didn't leave. Instead, he jumped down and walked over to Hattie. Out from behind his back came the pumpkin with the pie-shaped cut.

"For me?" Hattie asked. "But why?"

"A pumpkin with a hole is of no use to a peddler," the Pumpkin Man said. "Can *you* find a use for it?"

"Oh yes!" Hattie said. "Thank you." She ran inside to show Ma and Pa. And the pie-shaped cut…

made a *perfect* nose!

Ma's Blue-Ribbon Pie

3 eggs

2 cups of stewed pumpkin*

   (or 2 cups of canned pumpkin)

2/3 cup of brown sugar (packed firm)

1 2/3 cups of cream

1/2 teaspoon of salt

1 teaspoon of cinnamon

1 teaspoon each of ginger, cloves, and nutmeg

   (or 3 teaspoons of pumpkin-pie spice)

1 pastry shell, homemade or frozen

Preheat the oven to 425 degrees. Beat eggs, then beat in the remaining ingredients. Pour into a pastry-lined pie pan. Bake 15 minutes. Reduce oven temperature to 350 degrees and bake 50 minutes longer or until the pumpkin is firm. To test if the pie is ready, insert a knife in the middle. If it comes out clean, the pie is done.

*If you want to make pie fresh from the pumpkin, like Ma, here's how: Cut a small pumpkin in half and scrape out the seeds. Cut the pumpkin into slices, then cut off the rind. Chop each slice into cubes and boil in a small amount of water. As the pumpkin boils, stir often to prevent burning. After several hours, the cubes will be soft and mushy, like thick applesauce. Take out 2 cups for your pie and follow the recipe. (Keep the rest of the stewed pumpkin to serve on buttered bread with salt and pepper. Mmm good!)